STAR BRIGHT

Boris Zakhoder

Adapted by MARGUERITA RUDOLPH from the Russian

pictures by Stanley Mack

LOTHROP, LEE & SHEPARD CO./NEW YORK

Text copyright © 1969 by Marguerita Rudolph · Illustrations copyright © 1969 by Stanley Mack
Library of Congress Catalog Card Number: 70-81925 · Printed in the United States of America · All rights reserved

1   2   3   4   5   73   72   71   70   69

There once lived a toad, a clumsy-looking, homely creature who smelled of garlic and was covered with bumpy warts. BRR!

Fortunately, she didn't know what she looked like, or even that she was a toad, for she was still little and no one had ever called her by any name.

She lived in a garden with trees, shrubs, and flowers who talked only to those whom they loved. And you wouldn't call anyone you love "ugly toad" or even just "TOAD."

When the toad first came to the garden all the flowers were delighted that she didn't know her name.

"How lucky," said the bright-eyed Pansies who were the first to notice her. "We'll think of a name for you. If you like, we'll call you . . . Pansy."

But the Daisies spoke up quickly. "No, Daisy would be better."

"Beauty would be still better," said the Roses.

And the Bluebells said, "Ding-Dong, Ding-Dong,"
for those were the only words they knew.

The flowers would not have been able to decide on a name for the toad if it were not for the Asters and the Learned Starling.

"Let her be called Aster," said the Asters.

"Aster is another word for Star," explained the Starling, who knew many words. "Just look at her luminous eyes—they are bright as stars."

No one disagreed with the Learned Starling.

"Then let us call her Star Bright."

From then on everyone called the toad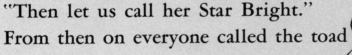

"What a star, indeed," hissed the sneaky Fat SNAIL. He had climbed onto the rosebush and was heading for the young, tender leaves. "Star, ha! She's nothing but an ordinary, common . . ." He didn't have time to say "toad," for at that moment Star Bright looked at him with her luminous eyes, and he disappeared.

"Thank you, my dear Star Bright," said Rose, recovering her bright color. "You saved me from a dreadful enemy."

Yes, even these innocent flowers had enemies—but luckily these enemies were tasty to a toad.

From the day Star Bright came to live in the garden the flowers bloomed from happiness.

"Come to us," called the Pansies.

"No, come to us first," called the Daisies.

Star Bright kept modestly silent. Only her eyes glowed with pleasure.

The Magpie, who was fond of eavesdropping on conversations, asked whether it was true that Star Bright had a precious stone hidden in her forehead. "Is that the reason that your eyes shine like stars?" she wanted to know.

But how could Star Bright answer? She had no idea what she looked like.

"Oh, that Magpie, how she blabbers!" scolded the Learned Starling. "Stone indeed. Star Bright has clear, luminous eyes because she has a clear conscience and does useful work. Doesn't that make sense?"

ENEMIES

The **ENEMIES** of the flowers did not think Star Bright so wonderful. The Greedy Bugs, the Caterpillars, and the Fat Snails hissed and called her bad names when she was out of sight.

"We don't feel safe in the garden any more," they complained among themselves. "We haven't tasted a Pansy or a Daisy or even a Bluebell since that ugly toad came along. It's just no life with her around."

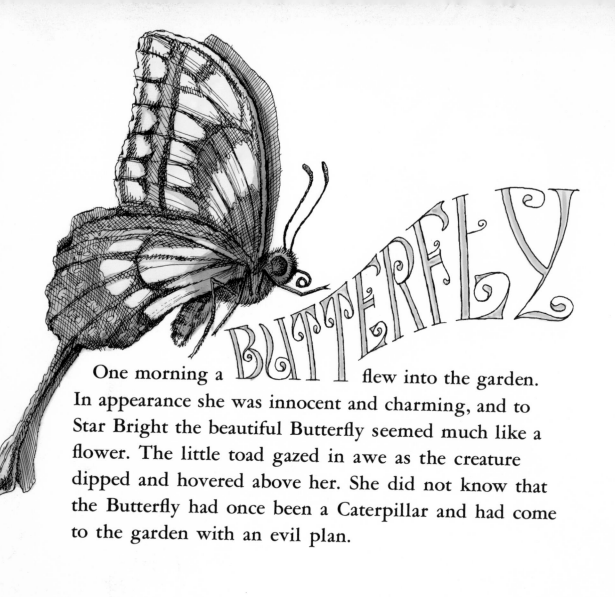

One morning a BUTTERFLY flew into the garden. In appearance she was innocent and charming, and to Star Bright the beautiful Butterfly seemed much like a flower. The little toad gazed in awe as the creature dipped and hovered above her. She did not know that the Butterfly had once been a Caterpillar and had come to the garden with an evil plan.

"I will soon rescue all of you from this dreadful toad," she told her sisters, the Caterpillars, and her friends, the Greedy Bugs and the Fat Snails.

For a time the Butterfly vanished from the garden but she soon returned with a SILLY BOY chasing after her. He was grasping his cap with one hand and waving it in the air, imagining that at any moment he'd catch the Butterfly.

The sly Butterfly kept pretending she was just about to be caught. She'd perch on a flower and ignore Silly Boy, then suddenly she would dart right under his nose and fly to the next clump. Thus, she was luring him deep into the garden, right to the path where Star Bright was sitting with the Learned Starling.

The Butterfly was instantly punished for her foul deed. The Starling flew down from the branch with lightning speed and grabbed her with his beak. But it was too late, for Silly Boy had already noticed Star Bright.

"TOAD!

Ugly toad!" Silly Boy screamed. And he lifted a heavy stone.

Star Bright didn't realize that he was talking about her—since she had never heard anyone call her "toad." She didn't move from her place even when Silly Boy swung the stone in her direction.

"Star Bright, get away!" called Starling in great alarm.

Fortunately, the heavy stone did not strike Star Bright. She quickly jumped aside and was hidden by the flowers and grasses.

But Silly Boy would not give up. He lifted more stones and threw them to the place where Star Bright was hiding. "Toad! Poisonous toad!" he yelled. "I'll get the ugly creature!"

"WHAT-A-FOOL," the Learned Starling called. "She is a friend who deserves our praise."

Silly Boy grabbed a stick and climbed into the rosebush to find Star Bright. But the sharp thorns of the rosebush stuck into him and Silly Boy ran out of the garden howling.

Star Bright sat alone by the roots of the rosebush and felt very sad. "He called me 'toad,'" she said to herself. "How UGLY I must be." And she wanted to hide from her friends in the garden.

They all tried to comfort her. The Pansies said
she would always be their darling Star Bright. The
Roses told her that beauty wasn't everything (which
was quite a thing for them to say!). And the Bluebells
whispered their comforting words, "Ding-Dong,
Ding-Dong. . . ."

But Star Bright could not hear them.

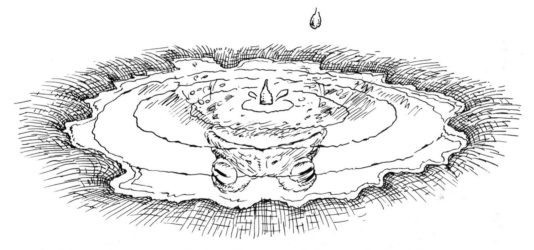

Only the Learned Starling understood that it was
still too soon to comfort Star Bright. "Let her be alone,
and let her cry until her own tears console her. She
will know that what a Silly Boy calls her is not
important."

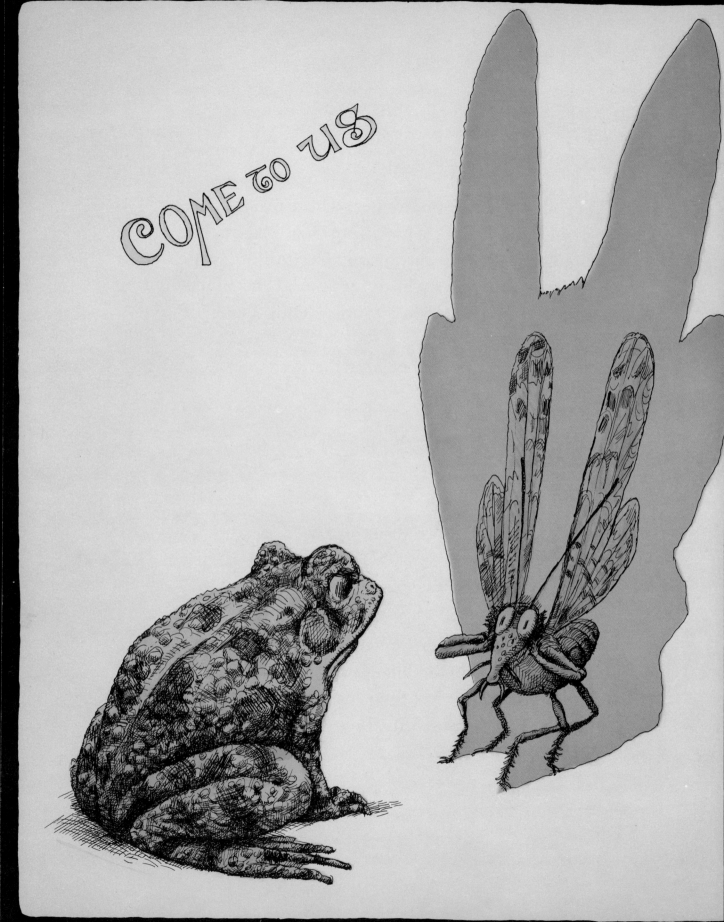

And Starling, of course, was right. For just as he spoke, a Greedy Bug approached the root where Star Bright sat, thinking she would not notice him. But in an instant her luminous eyes were upon him.

Suddenly the little toad wondered, "If I were not here, who would protect the flowers?" She had stopped crying and now could hear the voices of her friends.

"Come to us, Star Bright," the Pansies were calling.

"No, come to us first. . . ."

The little toad hopped out from beneath the rosebush.
For a moment she gazed round the beautiful garden
in which she lived. Then she set out to do her
evening's WORK.